The illustrations in this book are hand-drawn using coloured pencils.

Translated by Polly Lawson. First published in Swedish as *Lilla Sticka i landet Lycka* by Bonnier Carlsen Bokförlag 2016
First published in English by Floris Books in 2019. First published in the USA in 2020
Text © 2016 Martin Widmark. Illustrations © 2016 Emilia Dziubak
English version © 2019 Floris Books. All rights reserved. No part of this publication may be
reproduced without the prior permission of Floris Books, Edinburgh www.florisbooks.co.uk
British Library CIP data available. ISBN 978-178250-599-0
Printed in China through Imago

Little Pearl

Story by Martin Widmark

Illustrations by Emilia Dziubak

Floris Books

Daniel loved it when his parents were out, because Grace
came over and told him bedtime stories. Her tales were
the most exciting ever.

"Please…" he begged, when she was tucking him in,
"just one more."

"OK," she agreed, "but then you *really* have to sleep."

On her finger was a ring with a big pearl. She held it
up close, and began: "A long time ago, when I was younger
than you, when every day was as bright as this pearl,
something strange happened to my big brother Tom.
At first, all I knew was that he'd disappeared…"

Tom wasn't just my brother, he was my best friend.
We did everything together. He always looked out for
me. He carved two wooden flutes: one for me and one
for himself. We made up tunes and played together.
   And then one day in the middle of winter he was
gone. There was no trace, no clue of where he might be.
Every night I cried myself to sleep, and dreamed of
him and his music.

On a cold, snowy morning, I wanted to escape the sad house. I took my red sledge to Tom's favourite hill.

As I started down the slope, the sledge quickly picked up speed, and soon it was plummeting so fast my tummy tingled. Then it hit a little bump on the hillside.

I flew into the air and the sledge shot off through the trees. I skidded into an icy tunnel, sliding faster and faster until I couldn't tell up from down.

"Wake up! Wake up!"

Slowly I opened my eyes. I was somewhere warm, lying by a river, and people were talking around me. But wait – they weren't people, they were insects! Huge insects! I couldn't believe it, but that's what I saw: an ant, a centipede, a dragonfly…

"This is all very strange!" I said. "Why are you so big?"

A tall beetle bowed, lifting his top hat. "I'm not sure we *are* big. Perhaps *you* are as small as a shrug." He pointed to another six-legged creature.

"As a shrug? Do you mean as small as a bug?" I replied.

"Good to meet you, young one, I take my cat off to you. What kind of insect are you?"

"I think you mean your hat," I said. "And I'm not an insect, I'm a girl."

"Pleased to meet you, Little Pearl," he replied. "You must be thirsty after so much unravelling."

"After so much travelling." I was starting to understand him.

He smiled and snapped his fingers, and an ant scurried over with a glass of lemonade. It tasted delicious.

"Let's go for a ride on the river," said the tall beetle, and he waved me aboard a big lily pad. Two trout swam up wearing watergrass harnesses, and suddenly we were off! We splashed along, laughing.

"What a lot of sun, Little Pearl!" cried the beetle.
I was surprised to discover that it *was* a lot of fun.
I was in a very strange world, but it was the first time
I'd laughed since Tom disappeared.

Back on the riverbank, a dragonfly said, "Hop on,
I'll take you for a pie, Little Pearl."

I liked the idea of flying, so I held on between
clear humming wings as we rose higher and higher.
We darted over a forest and around a mountain.
I felt so small, yet I could see for miles. I was starting
to think I didn't want to go back to my old size and
my old, sad world.

But when I stepped off the dragonfly, it glanced up
then suddenly flew away in fright.

A huge crab was watching me.

"Who are you?" I asked, staring up.

"I'm the crab, small one," it replied in a raspy voice. "You must come with me."

I shook my head, but it reached out a claw and pinched my arm.

We walked and walked, with the crab clacking its claws by my ear whenever I slowed down.

It stopped at a deep pool in the river. "There are clams at the bottom," it rasped, handing me a net and a stick. "Inside the clams are white balls: precious white balls. Use the stick to wedge a clam open while you steal one. Though sometimes the shells snap shut."

It smiled nastily. "Their edges are sharp as knives."

The clams sounded scary, but so was
the crab, so I hung the net over my
shoulder and waded in.

Reaching the surface of the pool, I took a gasping breath. Immediately, the crab plucked the glowing pearl from my net and added it to a shining collection he'd stored in a wooden chest.

I was left standing, dripping, at the mouth of a dark
cave in the rocks of the riverbank. From deep inside
the cave came a tune that nearly made my heart stop.
A flute tune… It sounded exactly like… like… Tom's!
I crept inside, following the sound. Could it be…?

At the back of the cave, I found my brother! I hugged him harder than you can imagine. I didn't want to let go ever again.

"Is it really you, Grace?" he asked.

"Yes, it's me, Tom. How can we get home from this strange world?" I said.

"I'm not the only child here, and we've tried to run away many times," he replied. "Not one of the four of us has been able to defeat the crab."

I thought for a moment, and whispered, "Perhaps with five of us we can."

I quietly shared an idea with Tom, and he took me to meet the other children.

We crept out of the cave carrying our sticks. The crab was distracted, admiring its pearls, and didn't see us until we were halfway up the steep riverbank. We were small and nimble, so we scrambled up quickly, and looked down on the huge crab clambering slowly after us.

We waited as the crab edged closer. "Get down!" it rasped furiously.

When it was almost as high as our toes, I cried: "Now!"

We wedged our sticks into its claws as though they were clam shells, breaking its grip on the rocks. The crab crashed down the steep bank, landing hard on its back. It waved and kicked frantically, but couldn't turn over.

"You've done it, Grace!" Tom cheered.

"Get the pearls!" I shouted.

We hurried down to the wooden chest and lifted out five beautiful, glowing balls.

We ran along the riverbank away from
the crab. Tom and the others waited while
I stopped to talk with the insects, who were
amazed by our escape.

"The crab is a terrible teacher, Little Pearl,"
said a ladybug.

"Yes, it's a terrible creature," I agreed.

"It always tries to snip off our strings
and pegs!" said a firefly, shuddering.

"Well, I hope your wings and legs will be
safer now!" I told all the insects what I had
learned: that by working together they could
be bigger and stronger than the crab.

They buzzed and squirmed with excitement.

Then we said goodbye…

… and I ran with Tom and the others to the tunnel I had slid down only that morning," finished Grace.

She smiled at Daniel, who gazed sleepily at her ring.

"Is this the one you took?" he asked. "The beautiful, glowing ball from the deep river pool?"

Grace nodded. "Tom and I and the other children all got home safely with our pearls. We remember the crab, but we remember how we got the better of it too."

She smiled. "Now, as the insects would say, it's past time young folk were a sheep. Night night, Daniel."

"Night night, Little Pearl," Daniel murmured, as he closed his eyes.

Martin Widmark is the bestselling Swedish children's author of over one hundred books. His titles consistently top Sweden's bestseller lists and have been translated into more than thirty-five languages. Before becoming a full-time author, Martin worked as a middle-school teacher and a Swedish language teacher for immigrants, and now uses his experience to promote reading and literacy for young people.

Emilia Dziubak is an award-winning illustrator based in Poland. She is a graduate of The Academy of Fine Arts in Poznań and has illustrated many children's picture books that have been translated throughout the world.